Visit us on the Web!
rhcbooks.com
SesameStreetBooks.com
www.sesamestreet.org
Educators and librarians, for a variety of teaching tools, visit us at RHTeachersLibrarians.com
ISBN 978-1-5247-6415-9 (trade) – ISBN 978-1-5247-6718-1 (ebook)
Printed in the United States of America
10 9 8 7 6 5 4 3 2 1

Random House Children's Books supports the First Amendment and celebrates the right to read.

K Is for Kindness

By Jodie Shepherd

Illustrated by Tom Brannon

 A GOLDEN BOOK • NEW YORK

Elmo loved being a Monster Scout.
   He loved hanging out with the other scouts.
   He loved campfires and scout hikes and
scout singing.
   And he loved earning Monster Scout badges.

Elmo already had a Monster Music badge, a What's Cooking? badge, and a Be Good to the Earth badge. Now he was working on his K Is for Kindness badge.

"Elmo will have to work very hard to get the K Is for Kindness badge," Elmo told his mommy.

"You are a kind monster with a big heart," said Elmo's mommy. "That's a good start."

Elmo began that afternoon.

Elmo knew that step one was *Be kind to little monsters.*

Elmo looked around. He saw that his cousin Albie was crying!

"What's the matter, Albie?" Elmo asked.

"My car is broken," Albie answered, sniffing. "Look!"

"Phew!" said Elmo. "That's an easy one."
He gave Albie one of his own toy cars. "Elmo thinks this one is really cool."
Albie gave Elmo a hug.
"K Is for Kindness badge, here Elmo comes!" Elmo exclaimed.

Step two was *Be kind to older folks.*
Elmo looked around again. He saw Nani Bird
coming down the street and ran to greet her.
"You must be coming to
visit Big Bird," Elmo said.
"Let Elmo help you. . . ."

HOOPER'S STORE

"Thank you, Elmo," Nani Bird chirped cheerfully. "What a nice little monster you are!"

"That reminds Elmo," said Elmo.
After Nani Bird arrived at Big Bird's nest,
Elmo went inside and made a call.

"Hi, Grampa!" he said.

"Elmo!" boomed his grampa monster over the laptop. "It's always a sunny day when you call!" That made Elmo feel really good.

Be kind to animals was step three for earning the K Is for Kindness badge.
    The next day after school, Elmo helped Bert feed the pigeons.

Later, he helped the Count find a missing bat.
"That's one little lost bat, safely counted,"
said the Count. "Thank you, Elmo."

Help out a friend who is sick was step four. Grover had stayed home from school that day, so Elmo took some hot soup to his house.

"Chicken soup is just the thing for sneezy furry blue monsters," said Grover, who was snuggled in his bed. "*Aachooo!*"

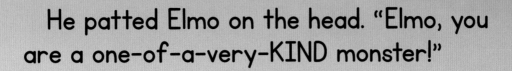

He patted Elmo on the head. "Elmo, you
are a one-of-a-very-KIND monster!"

Step five was *Be a good listener*, Elmo read in his Monster Scout handbook that night.

The next day was Saturday. Elmo went for a walk. And there was Abby Cadabby, coming his way. She looked sad.

"Hi, Abby," said Elmo. "What's the matter?"

Abby told him a long story about a magic spell gone wrong. Elmo listened quietly as she talked.

But when Abby finished speaking, she smiled. "Thanks, Elmo. I feel much better."

"But Elmo didn't do anything," said Elmo.

"You stopped and listened," said Abby. "You were a good friend."

Finally, for Elmo to earn his badge, he had to do just one more thing: *Turn a frown upside down.*

"Elmo knows who can help with that one!" Elmo exclaimed. He went downstairs and knocked on the lid of Oscar's trash can.

"Who's there?" said a grouchy voice.

"It's Elmo," replied Elmo.

"Oh, yeah? Well, get lost, fur-face," said Oscar, popping out.

"But Elmo needs to turn your frown upside down," explained Elmo. "It's for Elmo's Monster Scout badge. Now, let me see, what can Elmo do?"

Elmo gave Oscar a cupcake
with a pink heart on top.
Oscar frowned. "Yuck!
What's that?"

Elmo gave Oscar a big
yellow balloon.
Oscar frowned some
more. "Balloons are way
too cheerful," he said. "Until
they pop with a loud BANG!"

Elmo tried to give Oscar
a hug.
Oscar frowned even
more. "Grouches hate hugs!"

"Then how is Elmo going to change Oscar's frown into a smile?" he asked.

"Not possible!" Oscar said, laughing. "Grouches never smile."

Elmo looked sad. Then he looked at Oscar. "You're laughing!" Elmo said happily. "Elmo did it! Thank you, Oscar!"

"Oh, no! Don't mention it," grumbled Oscar. "I mean it. Really, *don't mention it*! Now scram!"

A few weeks later, there was a big party
to award the badges the Monster Scouts
had earned. Finally, it was Elmo's turn.

"Good job, Elmo," said the scout leader, giving Elmo his K Is for Kindness badge. "What did you learn?"

Elmo thought for a moment. "Elmo learned that being kind to someone else makes Elmo feel all warm and tickly inside," he answered. "It feels KIND of wonderful!"